Bring your baby to the library!

This book belongs to

Michael Warren Gardner

Reading to your child is a great
way to spend time together.
You can explore faraway lands,
meet children from long ago
or simply find a nice way to
say good night.

books*forbabies*

Sponsored by
Concord Public Library Foundation

March 19, 2008

For Rebecca Gray Wells
—T.T.

To my granddaughter "Spunken" Victoria
—H.S.

Wishes for You • Text copyright © 2003 by Tobi Tobias • Illustrations copyright © 2003 by Henri Sorensen • Manufactured in China.
All rights reserved. No part of this book may be used or reproduced in any manner whatsoever without written permission except in the case of
brief quotations embodied in critical articles and reviews. For information address HarperCollins Children's Books, a division of HarperCollins
Publishers, 1350 Avenue of the Americas, New York, NY 10019. • www.harperchildrens.com • Library of Congress Cataloging-in-Publication Data
Tobias, Tobi • Wishes for you / by Tobi Tobias ; illustrated by Henri Sorensen. •   p. cm. • Summary: A series of wishes for a child's bright and
hopeful future. • ISBN 0-688-10838-5 — ISBN 0-688-10839-3 (lib. bdg.) — ISBN 0-06-443730-2 (pbk.) • [1. Wishes—Fiction. 2. Family—Fiction.]
I. Sorensen, Henri, ill. II. Title. • PZ7.T56 Wi 2003 • [E]—dc21   2001024372 • Typography by Robbin Gourley and Jeanne L. Hogle •

Wishes for You

BY TOBI TOBIAS

ILLUSTRATED BY HENRI SORENSEN

HarperCollins*Publishers*

I hope you will have moments when you're so happy, you'll feel the sun is shining from inside you.

I hope you will have the strength and spirit
to deal with bad things
when they come your way.

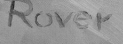

Rover

I hope you will be lucky.

I hope you will always be curious.

I hope you will never forget
how to be silly.

I hope you and I will have adventures together—
just the two of us.

I hope you will love to read.

I hope you will learn how to make things
with your own hands.

I hope you will want to make your body strong
and quick and beautiful—and enjoy the way that feels.

I hope you will love one special person
more than anyone or anything
in the whole world.

I hope that, one day when you're grown up,
you will have a child—different from you,
but just as wonderful.

I hope you will know what you think and feel and not let other people tell you.

I hope you will be able to tell your favorite people the secrets of your heart.

I hope you will always be part of a family.

I hope you will always remember me
and know how much I love you.